THE MOST SPECIAL BEAR

A special teddy bear helps a young boy
cope with grieving and the death of
his grandfather.

Special thanks to Kaye Eckert, Psy.D., Clinical Psychologist, for her insightful questions designed to draw out the young reader's feelings for discussion.

THE MOST SPECIAL BEAR

BONITA MASON, Author   **SANDY HENDRICKS**, Illustrator   **COLE MASON**, Graphic Design

Published By
PEACH BANDANA STUDIOS
Stoughton, Wisconsin

T-Bear The Most Special Bear

Peach Bandana Studios®

Stoughton, WI
www.peachbandana.com
Bonita.Mason@peachbandana.com
Sandy.Hendricks@peachbandana.com

Library of Congress Control Number: 2007937263

Mason, Bonita Mary.

T-bear, the most special bear / Bonita Mason, author ; Sandy
Hendricks, illustrator ; Cole Mason, graphic design. -- Stoughton, WI
: Peach Bandana Studios, c2007.

p. ; cm.

ISBN: 978-0-9798718-0-1

Audience: ages 4-12.
Summary: A special teddy bear helps a young boy cope with
grieving over the death of his grandfather. Includes a list of
questions by a clinical psychologist to draw out the child's feelings
for discussion. A sewing pattern is available for purchase for the
family to make their own special memory bear.

     1. Bereavement in children--Juvenile fiction. 2. Grief in children-
-Juvenile fiction. 3. Loss (Psychology) in children--Juvenile fiction.
4. Grandfathers--Death--Juvenile fiction. 5. Teddy bears--
Psychological aspects. I. Hendricks, Sandy. II. Mason, Cole.
I. Title.

Printed in China

DEDICATED TO

The Bear Lady, our Illustrator, Sandy Hendricks, who became a hospice volunteer after her mother spent her last weeks in a hospice facility. Sandy put her sewing and artistic skills together and started making cuddly teddy bears to comfort each patient.

When a friend died in a car accident, Sandy created a bear made from his favorite shirt for his nine-year-old daughter, Sarah, and thus began the "Memory Bear." Sarah later wrote in a thank-you-note, "Whenever I'm sad or depressed, I hold the bear and I feel better."

For a Pattern and instructions to make your own special Memory Bear, visit our website www.peachbandana.com.

Billy Joe reached over and adjusted the seatbelt on T-Bear's round middle. He squeezed the scruffy brown fur that was still a little damp. Mama had insisted on a thorough dunking in the wash machine before she would allow T-Bear to come along to see Papa. "I know you wouldn't give any germs to the old people," Billy Joe said. "Besides, old people like bears. Didn't Papa give you to me when I was sick and had to go to the hospital to get better?

"Papa always said, 'Thē most special bear for thē most special boy,'" Billy Joe giggled. "But I thought he said T-most special bear so I called you T-Bear. Anyway, now it's our turn to help Papa feel better."

The car pulled into the parking lot and Billy Joe's dad found a parking spot near the entrance to the new Hospice place where they had moved Papa. It wasn't big like the hospital.

There Billy Joe had to hold on tight to Mama's or Daddy's hand to find Papa's room. In this new place, he could skip down the hall and turn into the right room every time.

Billy Joe held T-Bear very gently around his middle. T-Bear's arms and legs dangled and flopped and one torn ear almost covered a smiling button eye.

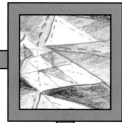

Papa was sleeping. He did that a lot now. Billy Joe tiptoed up to the bed and wedged T-Bear in bed next to Papa. He would be happy to see T-Bear. Papa never seemed to notice that T-Bear was all worn out from playing so hard with Billy Joe. Mama had stitched and stitched with a needle and thread, "Fighting a losing battle to keep body and soul together," she said.

Billy Joe thought it was more to keep stuffings in and arms and legs on. He wasn't sure what a soul was, but he thought it might have something to do with the smile that always hid in both T-Bear's and Papa's eyes.

While Mama and Daddy talked to the nurse, Billy Joe sat on the chair and watched carefully, waiting for Papa to open his eyes. Maybe this would be the day that Papa would feel strong again like he used to be when he'd throw Billy Joe way up in the air and then catch him just before he hit the ground. At first Billy Joe had been scared and cried like a baby. But Papa had hugged Billy Joe tight and said he'd never, ever, ever let Billy Joe fall and get hurt.

Papa was hurting now. Billy Joe could tell. The corners of Papa's mouth drooped down and hardly ever turned up in a smiley face any more. That's why Billy Joe brought T-Bear. T-Bear always made everybody smile.

"My, what a wonderful bear you have there." Billy Joe looked up. He had seen the same lady in the hall before, and she almost always carried a teddy bear.

"I was bringing this bear to the lady next door when I happened to peek in and see your friend visiting with your grandpa and thought we'd stop to say hello."

Billy Joe nodded. He wasn't supposed to talk to strangers. He couldn't help but notice the bear she was hugging. It was bigger than T-Bear and dressed in grandma clothes. It looked real nice. "Could you fix T-Bear to be like new again? My Mom says he's on his last leg."

The lady walked over to Papa's bed and looked T-Bear over carefully. "How about if I make you a new bear?"

"No, no, I don't think so." Billy Joe shook his head. "Papa gave T-Bear to me way back when I was little. I wouldn't want to hurt his feelings. Especially now when he is so sick."

The lady put her thumb under her chin, and finger along side her cheek, and seemed to think about that for a minute. "I am going to make a bear to keep your Papa company when you can't be here. What do you think that bear should look like?"

Billy Joe laughed. "That's easy. It should look like a T-Bear grown up."

"Why grown up?"

"Then it wouldn't chatter and bother Papa when he was sleeping, or run and skip in the halls." He looked up at the lady through his lashes, worried she'd think he was silly saying bears could do all that, but she still seemed to be listening.

The lady looked over at T-Bear, still tucked next to Papa in the bed. "So, maybe it should be a Papa Bear. What did you and your Papa like to do together?"

An achy feeling hurt in Billy Joe's chest. "Everything! I helped Papa work in the garden, planting all the flowers. He couldn't have done it without me to 'fetch and carry', he always said. He'd bring along a special bandana, just for me. He always bought two the same so mine could be just like his."

Billy Joe watched the lady take out a pen and note pad. "So, the Papa Bear should wear a bandana?"

Billy Joe nodded, "And suspenders. Papa always wears suspenders when he works. He bought me a pair one time, but they were too much trouble when I had to go to the bathroom in a hurry."

The lady's head bobbed, like she could understand that would be a problem. "Anything else?"

"Just jeans and a work shirt, I guess." Billy Joe looked over at the bed and wished Papa could get better so they could plant some flowers again. Then he remembered the most important thing. "And smiley eyes. The Papa Bear has to have smiley eyes."

The next time Billy Joe went to see Papa with Mama and Daddy, they told him he would have to be especially good because Papa was dying. They told him that Papa had lived a long and happy life, but that his body was worn out. But even though his body would die, his spirit would always be with them. He would always be a part of Billy Joe and be with him whenever he remembered all the good times they'd spent together.

Billy Joe knew about something wearing out. T-Bear was wearing out. He hoped the lady from the hospice could fix him. He had asked the bear lady to take T-Bear home to see what she could do.

When they got to Hospice, Billy Joe was careful to walk quietly down the hall. He was almost afraid to go into Papa's room. He wondered if the bear lady had fixed T-Bear.

He peeked around the corner of the door. It didn't look like Papa anymore.

Billy Joe walked slowly up to the bed and slipped his hand over Papa's. He squeezed it gently. "I love you, Papa."

He thought he felt a tiny squeeze back.

Then the life seemed to go out
of Papa and Billy Joe knew Papa
had died. Tears spilled down Billy
Joe's cheeks no matter how hard he
blinked.

He tried to remember exactly
what Mama had said about Papa's
spirit always being with him.

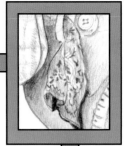

He glanced around the room, trying to keep from crying, until something caught his attention. There in the corner, sitting on top of the dresser, was the grown up T-Bear. He looked good as new but with the same old smiley eyes, just like Papa's.

The bear lady had remembered everything. The soft work shirt was surely made from one of Papa's old ones. The jeans were held up by blue suspenders, and a peach colored bandana poked through a belt loop. The peach bandana was Papa's and Billy Joe's favorite.

Billy Joe caught his breath. It could have been the shimmer from his own tears, but he swore he saw the bear wink. He cautiously let go of Papa's hand and ran to the dresser for a closer look.

He clutched the bear and hugged it tight, squeezing it like he'd been afraid to squeeze Papa since he'd been sick.

Then he held it away, looked deep into the smiley eyes….

. . . and winked back.

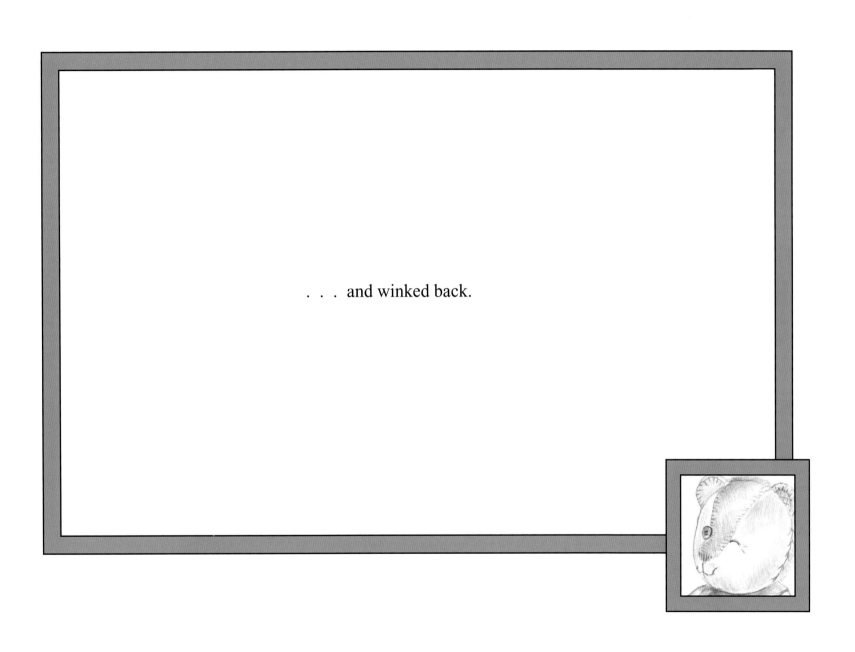

PSYCHOLOGIST'S NOTE FOR AN ADULT READING THIS BOOK TO A CHILD

Depending on age, children often react differently from adults when a family member dies. It is important for a child to have an opportunity to talk about his or her thoughts and to express feelings with an adult. There are many good resources available for helping children understand the dying process, learning about death practices such as funerals, and going through the grieving process. For example, the American Academy of Child and Adolescent Psychiatry website (www.aacap.org) contains helpful information under Resources for Families in "Children and Grief." The American Psychological Association's website (www.apa.org) contains recommended reading under Publications specifically written for children. Most libraries and bookstores offer books on the subject as well.

Some children are more verbal than others and able to talk things through while some find it easier to work through and express their feelings in art such as drawing, music or dramatic play. Often children find it easier to talk about deeper feelings when in natural settings or while doing something, such as while taking a walk or skipping stones across a pond or making a craft with an adult. These are ways that can be explored if a child has trouble dealing with grief.

For children who need additional help dealing with their grief, there are many professionals specifically trained in grief work, such as grief counselors employed by funeral homes, hospices, hospitals, and mental health clinics. These individuals and places can offer information about the range of resources available to you in helping your child.

To help provide an opportunity for your child to talk about the death of a loved one, I offer the following Questions For Discussion. I hope you find these to be a helpful addition to this beautiful story.

Kaye Eckert, Psy.D.
Clynical Psychologist

QUESTIONS FOR DISCUSSION

1)   What might Billy Joe have been thinking when he entered his grandfather's room and saw him looking so sick? What did you think or have you been thinking about?

2)   Billy Joe remembered so many good times with his grandfather. What things are you remembering about your times with _____?

3)   When someone we love dies, we have lots of feelings. For example, we might feel sad and we might even hurt. Some people feel cheated that the person is not in their life anymore or might even be angry with that person for dying. If a person is ill and suffering a long time, we might feel glad they die and are no longer hurting. There are lots of feelings and they are all OK. What kinds of ways are you feeling? (Note: for some children, it's easier for them to draw their feelings than to talk about them.)

4)   When you think of _____ , what is one thing you'll always remember about him/her?
     (Note: if the child has trouble thinking of something, offer some examples, such as, an important thing the person did, something learned from the person, a talent, an endearing trait, a quote, a favorite time.)

5)   Billy Joe now has T-Bear to remember his grandfather. T-Bear is wearing clothes and a bandana like his grandpa wore when he and Billy Joe gardened together. What can you think of doing or of having that will bring back good memories of _____?
     (Note: This provides an opportunity for a child to have something tangible to keep the loved one's memory alive. It might be an activity such as planting a tree or making a scrapbook or picture collage. Or it might be asking for an item the loved one owned such as a piece of jewelry, medal, a handmade item, a key chain, Bible or favorite book, piece of music, etc.

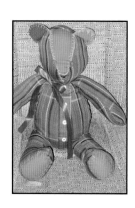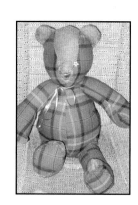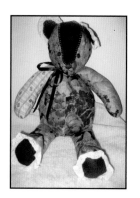

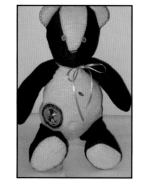

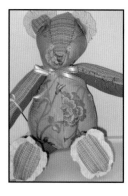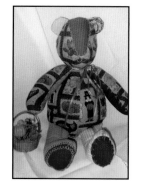

To order a pattern and directions
to make your own special Memory Bear,
please visit our website at:

www.peachbandana.com

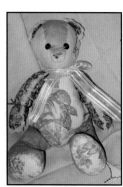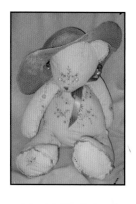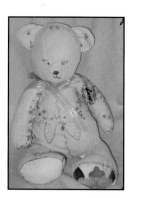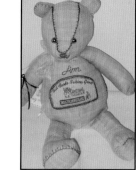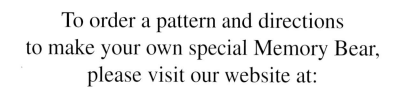

TESTIMONIAL

"T-Bear is a gift for children, especially those who have lost or are knowingly or unknowingly losing someone they love very much. We live in an era when more and more parents know that it is important to be honest about all of life, the pains and sorrows as well as the pleasures and joys. We are learning to be truthful and open about death and dying as a part of life, something that is natural and not to be feared. Many of us have experienced great beauty and meaning and joy in walking with a loved one in the final stages of his or her life, and we want to help our own children to be open to such experiences as well. That is the gift that this lovely book helps us give our children.

On the simple level, the book helps us to understand what a hospice facility is, how it is separate and different from a hospital. Hospice is shown as a caring place where a person can be comfortable and nurtured during serious illness and the time of dying.

Secondly, the book allows children to recognize the changes a person they love experiences when dying, even though those changes may be very small from day to day. The ability for children to know and understand that changes occur helps them in the dying and grieving process.

Thirdly, the book allows children to recognize the comfort needed for those who are dying. In a touching moment, the child gives the teddy bear which has comforted him to his grandfather. Children are highly perceptive when someone they love is hurting, and this book permits the boy to share his feelings and his own need for comfort naturally.

Finally, with the understanding that loved ones do not die from our memories, Bonita Mason and Sandy Hendricks assist all of us as we grieve the loss of someone so dear to us. Creating a ritual for remembrance (here the newly refurbished bear) shows a child how to keep memories close to heart. They help us, as parents, grandparents and godparents to speak of our own faith and faith traditions and what we believe about death to this life.

May T-Bear be a gift to your family in this poignant time of life."

James L. Jelinek, Bishop The Episcopal Diocese of Minnesota

TESTIMONIALS

"I have read T-Bear. It is well written and very appropriate for young readers dealing with death and loss."
Linda Perella, APSW Grief Counselor

"Spiritually sound."
K. Labinski, Hospice Chaplain

"So consoling, heartwarming and true-to-life perfect for youngsters who have experienced the final days and loss of a loved one. Seems everything was covered and so well done. Thanks for everything."
Pat Baus, Relative of hospice patient

"Praise and thank you to Bonnie Mason and Sandy Hendricks for their presentation of a very emotional subject to children. Graceful words and tender illustrations depict the dying process and help a child learn that even death need not mean the end of someone we love. Those who help children and their families cope with tough life experiences are very grateful for this healing resource."
Kaye Eckert, Psy.D., Clinical Psychologist

"The Most Special Bear" is a realistic, yet heartwarming story for parents and children about the times we need to love and let go. The subject of death is addressed from the viewpoint of a child and especially valuable is the appendix of questions parents can use to get the child to express his/her feelings. It's a book to be treasured."
Cathie Barns, Children's Librarian

"T-Bear is a comforting, quiet book that offers parents a good starting point to talk about grief with their children."
Erlene Bishop Killeen, School Librarian

Bonita Mason has been a life-long resident of Wisconsin. Reading developed into a passion at the age of six when she discovered books and expanded into writing while still in grade school. She is the mother of three sons and a daughter, as well as the grandmother of seven. She attended and graduated from the University of Wisconsin Madison as an adult student with a great deal of support and cooperation from her husband, Wally, and their four young children. She took every creative writing class available while attending the University and has completed several novels.

Bonita and Sandy Hendricks met and discovered their mutual interest in children's literature while working together on a Habitat for Humanity build with their spouses and later helping with the Katrina clean-up in Mississippi.

Bonita was inspired to write the story, T-Bear, by the selfless dedication of Sandy, "The Bear Lady," who had been looking for a way to help young relatives of hospice patients understand and cope with the death of a loved one.

Sandy Hendricks was also born and raised in Wisconsin. She graduated from the Layton School of Art in Milwaukee and later moved to Colorado where she met and married her husband, Jon. They raised their seven children there and now have seven grandchildren.

After retiring in 2000 and moving back to Wisconsin, she began the Angel's Grace Hospice bear program. She now has help from other volunteers, but Sandy has personally made over a thousand bears for hospice patients. Children's literature always interested her and illustrating a children's book was a long time dream.